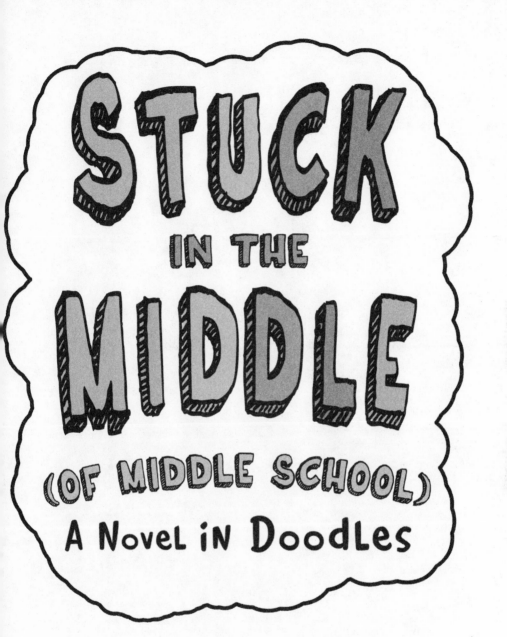

STUCK IN THE MIDDLE

(OF MIDDLE SCHOOL)

A Novel in Doodles

KAREN ROMANO YOUNG

FEIWEL AND FRIENDS
NEW YORK

For my sweet, encouraging, singing, doodling kids:

Bethany,

Samuel Gordon,

and Emily

Rock Stars!

★ With special thanks to Faye ★

A FEIWEL AND FRIENDS BOOK
An Imprint of Macmillan

STUCK IN THE MIDDLE (OF MIDDLE SCHOOL). Copyright © 2013 by Karen Romano Young. All rights reserved.
Printed in the United States of America by R. R. Donnelley & Sons Company, Crawfordsville, Indiana.
For information, address Feiwel and Friends, 175 Fifth Avenue, New York, N.Y. 10010.

Library of Congress Cataloging-in-Publication Data Available

ISBN: 978-0-312-55596-2 (hardcover) / 978-1-250-03765-7 (ebook)

Book design by Kathleen Breitenfeld

Feiwel and Friends logo designed by Filomena Tuosto

First Edition: 2013

10 9 8 7 6 5 4 3 2 1

mackids.com

1. Tighty Whitey

THINGS are good. are great!

Elizabeth Kaur / Colleen Callahan or, as she is known in these parts, the COOTIE CATCHER, is telling Momo's fortune with her paper-folding arts.

"You will become a world-famous opera singer, Maureen."

"NAH, I'm going to be a ROCK STAR."

And Mom says, "That's Momo for ya. She never settles."

In the kitchen, Magic Marco Pinho says, "you mean, nothing's ever good enough for her?" (HIS CHEEKS ARE EVEN PINKER THAN WHEN HE GOT HERE, AND THAT WAS ALREADY PRETTY PINK!)

"Not a bit!" says Dad. "She doesn't let what anyone else says or does LIMIT her."

And then he makes a great proclamation:

"EVERYBODY SHOULD MAKE THEIR own STOP SIGNS IN LIFE."

"Hooray for that idea but isn't it time to get going?

This is the reason we are all here together at our house. All together, we are going to witness MOM'S big cottony moment:

We dropped M.M. and C.C. off on our way home.

Magic Marco   Cookie Catcher

Marco

lives in a tall, modern apartment house on top of the HIGHEST hill.

"SWANKY!" says Mom.

Bye! Thanks!

Bye Marco!

Elizabeth

lives in the cutest cottage in a long row of cute cottages. "Cute, but crowded," she says.

"If only I was an only child."

But she has 4 sisters.

Bye! See you tomorrow!

Bye Cookie!

"That's a SWEET house," says Dad.

"What does his father do?" asks Dad.

"He's a graphic artist," says Elizabeth.

"Oh, so it CAN be done!" says Mom.

Dad didn't answer.

"It doesn't take a lot of money to be happy," says Mom.

There was a silent space in the car.

"Well, that's good!" said Mom. "Since we don't have a lot of MONEY."

I said, "Yeah, well, pretty soon, TIGHTY WHITEYS will be on all the big shots in the city!!"

MOMO said, "You mean all the Big Butts!!"

Mom said, "From your 👄 to God's 👂."

I asked, "What will you buy?"

Mom said, "A SWEET little house."

DAD said, "No, a SWANKY apartment."

MOMO asked, "Can we take SVEN?"

And we all answered, "Sven is Staci's cat."

Momo said, "Maybe he is just a little bit ours?"
If EVERYTHING around here feels like
it is just a little bit ours, that is
because we have tried to make it so.
By now it is ALMOST our house, our apartment,
our stairs, our neighborhood, our roof, our cat,
our city, our school, our life. But guess what?

Staci comes home in just 3 days.

We are maybe moving into a little house near
the Cootie Catcher's cute cottage. It is for rent.

Yes, sir! We are staying.

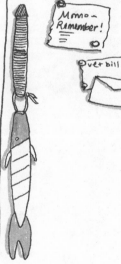

DAD is still interim manager for now.

MOM's underwear is all over the city. Hee hee.

MOMO has a solo in the choir's spring concert.

AND ME?

I am the UNSTOPPABLE, AMAZING,
TROUBLESHOOTING, BRILLIANT,
THRILLING, CHILLING, KILLING......
(turn the page!)

And Sven comes out and
listens to us when we talk,
but still won't let us pet him.

Of course, Cootie Catcher was talking about my

Fabulous Page,

which has, so far:

- ☆ iPod division
- ☆ coloradoodle
- ☆ graph how-to
- ☆ study helps
  - ▶ Venn diagram
  - ▶ cootie catcher
  - ▶ sound waves

S.F. SCHOOLS

OUR SCHOOL

LINX...

GALLERY

April Fool Hop!

- HOMEWORK HOT
- EXTRAS
- FABULOUS PAGE

"THANKS, COOTIE!"
I said. "There's lots more
to come. There's gonna be a
timer, a schedule, a
decision-maker (sort of magic
8 ball), plus spelling disasters
and a podcast and movies
and ..."

"AND AND AND STOP!!"
said Cootie Catcher.
(There it was again, the
Stop Sign in Life.)

STOP

It's on the school web site: FAME!

 WHAT?

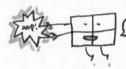 HOP!

The great big BURST on
the bottom! where it
says April Fool Hop!

"What's the April Food Hop?" I asked. I swear, there is
always some crazy new thing to deal with at this school!

"FOOL, fool!" said C.C. "It's a dance, young lady."

"Will there be food?" I asked. "In our old school in L.A.
they had discos and the best part was the
marshmallow fights."

"Here, the best part is the BOYS," said Cootie.
Then she asked,

"Are you going to go with MAGIC MARCO?"

We didn't look at each other, we looked out the window. It was easier that way. Mom tried not to pry, and I tried not to have a **tantrum**. It wasn't what you'd call an easy conversation and we could only hope Dad and Momo were iPodding again. "MOMO, YOU'D BETTER NOT BE LISTENING."

to what?

We talked softly so she couldn't. Mom said, "You could ask Marco, you know, Dodo."

I said, "What the heck is the point of a double date?"

"Makes it easier sometimes," said Mom. "You're not stuck with just one person trying to talk."

"Do I HAVE to?" I asked. "Just because the Cootie Catcher wants to?"

"Does it have to be a big deal?" said Mom. "I mean, you'd probably go with the two of them anyway. They're your best friends. Just like you brought them tonight."

"That was COOL," I said. "I'd rather just have it be Cootie. WHY does she have to bring this Waldo guy?"

WALDO!! said Momo. "GET OUT OF HERE!"

I yelled. GRRRRRRR.

trudge   trudge

pro	con

 Elizabeth Kaur, also known as Colleen Callahan, also known as **Cootie Catcher**

 I'm into paper.

 Ms. Farley and her **anti-doodling** policy. Bleh!

F fail! fizzle! fooey! flunk! freak-out! flop! feh! flub!

MR. HILL!!! I'm a fan!

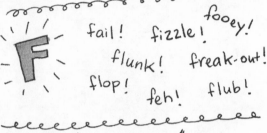 -**detention**-

 ★ **Magic Marco,** and his marker connection

 **Fifth-graders** with **peanuts** for brains!!

 Lunch.

2. SCHOOLY-SCHOOL

The next morning...

SOME THOUGHTS ON MS. FARLEY

She doesn't like me. She's the only one of my teachers that doesn't like at least SOMETHING about me. And, if you know what I mean, she dislikes me even more because my other teachers like me.

What'm I going to do, Doodlebug?

Have you expressed your horror?

NAW. How can I, when he's all happy and psyched? He doesn't know what she's like.

Do you think she likes him?

YEAH. Why wouldn't she? She was just sitting there staring at the view....

The beauteous view.

And you know, Dad's got money, and he's a hottie.

Who says, HIM? (Like father, like son.)

←This is what Marco and I were talking about while we left the stairs and went to homeroom. I guess we were kind of WHISPERING, which is fun for Elizabeth when it's her, but when it's me, she gets annoyed. As soon as I sat down in Spanish (after being walked there by Marco, who takes German) a balloon landed on my desk.

I popped it.
I palmed it. I uncrunched it and read it:

POW!

Did he ask ya?

The Flat Balloon

(Watch out, Cootie Catcher. This could be YOU next!)

Then I made my own balloon

1.   2.   3.

4.   5.   6.

7.   8.   9.

"Why do you call her that?" I asked.

> All that glitters is not gold. said Mr. Hill. It was quite a statement.

WHAM! POW! WHACK!

I kept on wedging clay, which is a good way to get air bubbles out of the clay and to get steam out of my system, and which has saved my sanity PLENTY.

Elizabeth pulled my crumpled F (for failure, Farley, and Farkle) out of my notebook and showed my political cartoon.

Doreen Bussey
Social Studies
period 3

Kiddie Porn

Kitty Porn
We're all the same under our fur

I don't think girls' magazines should have so much stuff about attracting boys in them. Last week I checked some of the covers of the most popular magazines. If I had bought them I could have found out how to bake cookies boys would like or how to be a better kisser, and that's not

"That's not all," I said. "There were six more pages." I quoted the covers of the big magazines and compared them with magazines for boys.

"And?" asked Mr. Hill. "Forgive me but I am not that familiar with what the girl guides are putting out there."

"Simple," said Elizabeth. "If you want to know where to go and what to do and how to do it, read a boy mag. If you want to know what to wear, pick up Thirteen or Lioness or Personality or whatever."

"So what was Ms. Farley's problem with all this?" asked Mr. Hill.

I said,

"A. It was supposed to be a summary of a current event, not a commentary on a trend.

B. She didn't ask for visuals."

Elizabeth said, She's a Farkle!

Mr. Hill said, "Sparkle Farkle."
when we left, she asked me, Should he have called another teacher a name?
(Cootie Catcher can be tricky this way.)
I said, "Mr. Hill is a good EGG."

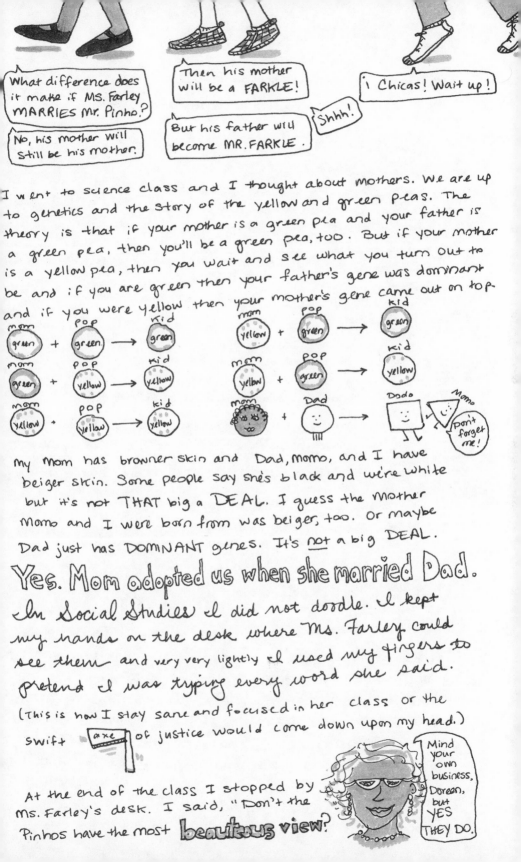

What difference does it make if MS. Farley MARRIES Mr. Pinho?

No, his mother will still be his mother.

Then his mother will be a FARKLE!

But his father will become MR. FARKLE.

Shhh!

Chicas! Wait up!

I went to science class and I thought about mothers. We are up to genetics and the story of the yellow and green peas. The theory is that if your mother is a green pea and your father is a green pea, then you'll be a green pea, too. But if your mother is a yellow pea, then you wait and see what you turn out to be and if you are green then your father's gene was dominant and if you were yellow then your mother's gene came out on top.

mom (green) + pop (green) → kid (green)

mom (green) + pop (yellow) → kid (yellow)

mom (yellow) + pop (yellow) → kid (yellow)

mom (yellow) + pop (green) → kid (green)

mom (yellow) + pop (green) → kid (yellow)

mom + Dad → Dodo Momo (Don't forget me!)

My mom has browner skin and Dad, Momo, and I have beiger skin. Some people say she's black and we're white but it's not THAT big a DEAL. I guess the mother Momo and I were born from was beiger, too. Or maybe Dad just has DOMINANT genes. It's not a big DEAL.

Yes. Mom adopted us when she married Dad.

In Social Studies I did not doodle. I kept my hands on the desk where Ms. Farley could see them and very very lightly I used my fingers to pretend I was typing every word she said.

(This is how I stay sane and focused in her class or the swift axe of justice would come down upon my head.)

At the end of the class I stopped by Ms. Farley's desk. I said, "Don't the Pinhos have the most beauteous view?

Mind your own business, Doreen, but YES THEY DO.

I was :SHOCKED:

(yes, MS. Farley had still been obnoxious to me.

but, she had also smiled and "connected" with me.)

WHOA, NELLIE!

At lunch, I told Marco and Cootie Catcher what

MS. Farley had said.

"maybe she is about to be transformed by love," I said.

"Like someone else I know!" said the Cootie Catcher.

WHO???

marco's face got those pink spots. Mine, too, I guess.

The wild wacky Momo landed at our lunch table.

PLOP! went her tray on the table.

"Who wants half a Twinkie?" Everyone did.

I said into her ear, "Are all the FIFTH GRADE tables full?"

What with the half Twinkies and everything, Momo is popular enough at our little SEVENTH GRADE table. But why.... ?

1/2 + 1/2 + 1/2 + 1/2 = 2 whole TWINKIES yum! But why?

And then, the most embarrassing thing ever:

Cootie catcher remembered her mission

to get me and Marco to go to the April Fool Hop.

She did not come right out and say it. She just started talking about her angelic cousin Waldo again.

"He has size THIRTEEN feet * and he can MOONWALK like that old Michael Jackson video. It's his karaoke specialty."

"Michael JACKSON!" said Momo. "Ancient HISTORY! Our FATHER can moonwalk." That is the shameful truth.

"So, he can DANCE, and dancing is BIG in Palo Alto!!!"

"COOL, ELIZABETH," I said.

* Hint: that size is, like, bigger than this whole book.

Then **Momo** looked up at me and honestly, she was just curious, and asked,

Are *you* going to the dance, Dodo?

But Elizabeth acted like someone in one of those magazines and shot Marco her elbow and said,

Well, she'd LIKE to, wouldn't you, Doodlebug?

OW! What?

I decided it was time Elizabeth experienced the great

stop sign STOP of life

and so I said, with extra-wide eyes and my giantest smile,

YEAH, I was thinking we could do like last night and pick up Marco first, then you and Waldo, and all go together.

Okay. Elizabeth was stunned but pleased. That shut her up.

Okay. I don't know what Marco thought, but he didn't object.

Me, too?

Uh-oh to Momo.

Aren't any of *your* friends going?

You see, if we drove Marco, Elizabeth, and Waldo, there wouldn't be enough room for Momo in the car, too.

And that's when I realized what was going on with our little **Momo** and started wondering,

ARE all the fifth grade tables FULL?

or what?

A Theatrical Chapter

3. Family Drama

Was I sympathetic to Momo?

being alone.

W E L L L L...

Heck yeah, I was sympathetic. Here was Momo, who had to leave our old school because of something I did, her old school where she had these three best friends who were so besty they all had the same pizza charms on their charm bracelets and Mom called them the yayas, after some besty four friends in an old book.

Hershey kiss

Schoolbus Peter Rabbit locket

yaya pizza

Piggy bank + penny

10
10th bday

American Girl doll

She has extra space for more charms.

So I was nice to Momo when Elizabeth and/or Marco came over. I didn't exactly have a choice because it's not like I even have my own bedroom and we're not allowed up on the roof without ADULT SUPERVISION.*

Maybe if we rent the sweet little S.F. cottage I will have my own space but meanwhile what is Momo supposed to do, sit in the bathroom and read a book when I have a friend or two over?

*If they have such supervision why do they have to be there in person? JOKE. Hahaha. Good one.

was I kind?

uhhhhhhhhh.......

At first maybe I was. Yesterday, when Marco and Elizabeth both came over, Marco and I were doodling while Elizabeth was telling Momo's fortune. So what was my problem today?

It was just Elizabeth. You can't think she would just let me go home without some explanation about MARCO and DATES and WALDO.

BUT NOW LOOK!! or should I say listen:

Cootie Catcher the famous *soprano* and Miss Maureen Bussey the big-whoop *alto* were in the echo-ey bathroom * Singing.

was I annoyed? YES!!!

Whose friend WAS Cootie Catcher anyway?

Who had even given boring old Elizabeth Kaur that cool name?

Wasn't she here to see ME? ME? ME?

Didn't she want to tell me more of the WONDERS of WALDO?

(Didn't she want to brag me some more about Magic Marco?)

And what about that BRAT RAT Momo?

What was GOING ON here?

Did Momo think she was so great for her singing, and did she think Cootie was great for _her_ singing, and was she feeling SUPERIOR to me for my non-singing?

Did Momo think she was too Cool for School—

fifth grade school, that is—

and had she elected herself an honorary member of the seventh grade?

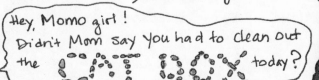

Hey, Momo girl!
Didn't Mom say you had to clean out the CAT BOX today?

How rude!

Sven lay back his ears and looked peeved.

Strangely enough, it was not the singing that got to me. It was not that Elizabeth was not asking me about Marco. (I didn't want to talk about him anyway, now did I, even though I thought maybe now that he and I were going with her and Waldo, it was MISSION ACCOMPLISHED for them— that TRICKY Cootie Catcher!) It was when she asked Momo,

"So, are you guys going to move into that house on my street?"

Of all the things that is the one that made me say Elizabeth, you're supposed to be MY friend. So why don't you ask me that???

Before anyone could even answer, Mom poked her head in from the kitchen. Maybe with all the music we hadn't heard her come into the apartment. Or maybe she had been just plain EAVESDROPPING. She said,

Funny you should ask, miss Cootie Catcher! I'm hoping to go over and sign the lease TONIGHT! Girls, I just left a message with the landlord.

FANTASTIC!!

We all went crazy and for a while nobody seemed to notice that I'd gotten mad.

BECAUSE, which of us Busseys has not dreamed of a sweet little house —

EVEN IF none of us Busseys ever said so, it is what we all wanted.

even a rented, not owned house — in San Francisco?

Everything was coming true.

EVEN IF I'd got thrown out of L.A. school, I LOVED MY S.F. school.

EVEN IF I got mad at Cootie Catcher Elizabeth sometimes, I LOVED HER and it would be cool to live near her.

EVEN IF I was sick of the loud music, NOW we all put on the CD again and ROCKED OUT.

Hey! What's all this unbridled joy?

WE'RE MOVING TO ELIZABETH'S STREET!

We had walked to the sweet little cottage, but now Mom headed to the bus stop so we wouldn't have to make the long climb back up the hill to Staci and Sven's apartment. All of a sudden I was a little sad, thinking of Sven and our cozy place by the big pine tree. Also I had a nervous-stomach feeling about Mom and Dad. ~~MOMO~~ chattered like a ~~monkey in the treetops~~ about the cottage and under her BLABBING, I listened to Mom and Dad.

FOR SHORT

Jolene — I'm Jo
Doreen — I'm Do
maureen — I'm mo
warren — Wo is me.

"But Jo, we weren't going to sign a year lease until BOTH our situations were SOLID."

"Warren, we have to keep Dodo and Momo in this school district."

"At what risk? Nothing we're doing is reliable work."

Wo, there's something I haven't told you.

Wow! What's more RELIABLE than TIGHTY WHITEYS?

My "Moon over S.F." campaign is going national!!!

Let's Celebrate!

We went into a COFFEE SHOP to get dinner. That's when Dad realized

o mom hadn't intended to wait for him to sign the lease. She was going to do it while he worked late.

o Nobody had fed Sven.

o He didn't feel like eating. Or waiting.

Moon over America!

DAD SAID, "You ladies enjoy. I'll head home to the ~~kitty~~ cat. Bring me a slice of chocolate cake, will ya?"

The bus didn't come for Dad yet.

BUS

SURPRISE! You didn't realize you were wearing underwear! So comfy-cozy It's barely there.

TIGHTY WHITEY

Dad waited for the bus for a little while. Right about the time I got my grilled cheese and tomato sandwich he gave up and started walking. I managed two bites, and then I went after him.

Mom said, "Dodo! You can't walk home alone!"

I said, "I'll catch up with Dad. He's right there." She didn't even know! She thought he'd caught the bus! Her back had been to the window the whole time and she'd never turned to check! What was THIS all about? I ran after Dad, but then the bus went past me. I saw him turn, and then he got lost behind the bus, and I figured he waved it down and got on it. I would have to turn back to Mom and Momo.

BUT NO, when the bus took off, there was Dad, still heading up the hill. I thought,°°°

He wants to be alone.

So I just followed behind him all the way home.

And I thought,°°°

What's his problem? It's not like he's been fired.

But it's not like he's been HIRED, either. And Mom's going NATIONAL.

F.Y.I.* When your Dad cries, it isn't good. Ever.   * for your information

I said, "It's just a one-year lease. It's still kind of 'interim.'"
Interim is the word Mom and Dad used when we came to S.F.

"It's not **permanent**" → (is a word that doesn't seem to have anything to do with my family, so far.)

PERMANENT MARKER
SUPER Pointy

I cannot be erased.

I can't resist saying I was worried Dad was flipping his lid.

Wheel!

I was sad for him, and scared, but I didn't think there was anything REALLY wrong. How could it be, when we were getting a cottage and staying at our good school, and OUR underwear moon ad was going all over the U.S.A.?

In case you forgot (I sure wish I could), Dad is just the interim manager at his work. We came from Lolo to S.F. for this work. Dad was very excited about his new job of graphic designer, plus we needed to move because of an idiotic antic of mine that got me EXPELLED.

Yes, you've got it: I feel guilty about making us move. And Dad is the one who made it work, finding the graphic designer job and borrowing his art-school friend Staci's apartment while she is in Japan. Staci will be home **WEDS.** and this is already **MON.**

I said, "Dad, can we have a man-to-man talk?" This is what we sometimes do even though only one of us is a man.

Dad blew his nose.

once   twice   Okay, Doodlebug.   You the man.

I said,

1. You're the one who said we'd better get **cracking.**
2. I'm the one with the friend who knew the little house was for rent.
3. Staci is the person making us move out.

SO why are you mad at Mom?"

Dad said,

You're absolutely right, Dodo. I guess it's just that I wanted to be the ~~hero~~. Instead, I'm still waiting for good news.

So he was just jealous! Well I understood that. But it didn't stop the fight he had with Mom that night.

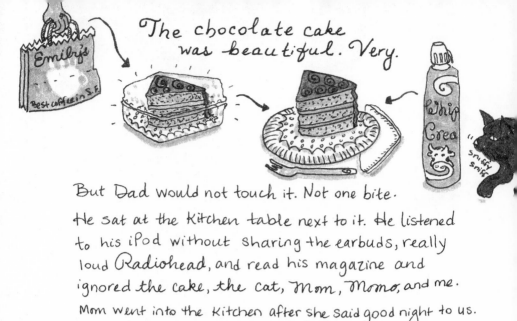

The chocolate cake was beautiful. Very.

But Dad would not touch it. Not one bite.

He sat at the kitchen table next to it. He listened to his iPod without sharing the earbuds, really loud *Radiohead*, and read his magazine and ignored the cake, the cat, Mom, Momo, and me.

Mom went into the kitchen after she said good night to us.

WO, YOU'RE RIGHT. I SHOULD HAVE TOLD YOU FIRST, BUT WE STILL HAD TO SIGN THAT LEASE.

I THINK IT'S IRRESPONSIBLE. THAT UNDERWEAR CAMPAIGN'S NOT GOING TO GO ON FOREVER.

NO, BUT IT'LL LEAD TO OTHER WORK. THIS IS A GOOD THING FOR ALL OF US, WARREN. AND IT'S GREAT FOR DODO TO SEE IT COME FROM HER CONCEPT. PLUS I'M NOT THE ONLY WORKER IN THE HOUSE.

MAYBE YOU SHOULD BE. MAYBE I'M NOT MOTIVATED ENOUGH.

WO, HONEY, WHAT ARE YOU SAYING?

I DON'T KNOW. SHHH... THE GIRLS!

And that is when Mom dragged him out into the stairwell so we couldn't hear. It's not like they were yelling, just talking really, really seriously. Not mad. Sad.

MOMO cried. I rubbed her leg with my foot, and turned over and shut my eyes and said the alphabet over and over until sometime during the fourth time I fell asleep.

Naturally, under such circumstances, I sleep-walked. I found myself in the kitchen as usual. (Will I end up in the kitchen if I sleepwalk at the new house?)

By the light of the Statue of Liberty nightlight Dad bought so I wouldn't turn on the stove light at night, I wrote him a note and told him it was all going to be O.K.

But the next morning he got on a train and went back to Los Angeles

Is he coming back?

Accidentally the angel I drew came out looking like Momo, so I made her saying what Momo said.

Mom said, "What are you thinking?"

We were thinking of Dad traveling back all the way we came

3 incredibly long months ago.

I was thinking of Dad maybe wanting his L.A. job back.

Mom said, "He is just going to get a U·HAUL truck and get our stuff out of storage and drive back here. He'll be back on Friday night. In the meantime we'll move everything in from here and go to IKEA and welcome Staci home and—"

Goodbye!

ALL RIGHT! We get it! What do you think, Mom, we're STUPID or something?

4. Adjectives of the Day (hooray)

- ☑ red hot
- ☑ cool
- ☑ embarrassed
- ☑ tardy
- ☑ visual
- ☑ intelligent
- ☑ private

By the time I reached my first destination of the day, the principal's office, my cheeks felt **RED HOT** and my eyes were full of tears. The door to **MS. WU's** office was closed, but **Mr. Stein**, her secretary, was there in his usual spot, his desk. He took one look at me and said, "Have a seat, Doodlebug." He held his finger to his lips  and whispered, "She's in an IMPORTANT "MEETING." So I just handed him the note Mom had written to the school telling when we were moving and what our new address was going to be. I stood up to go, but he waved me back into the chair.

"What's wrong?" he whispered. He held his fingers to his lips again, and passed me his yellow legal pad and a pen. For a few moments we wrote back and forth, then he wrote a late pass

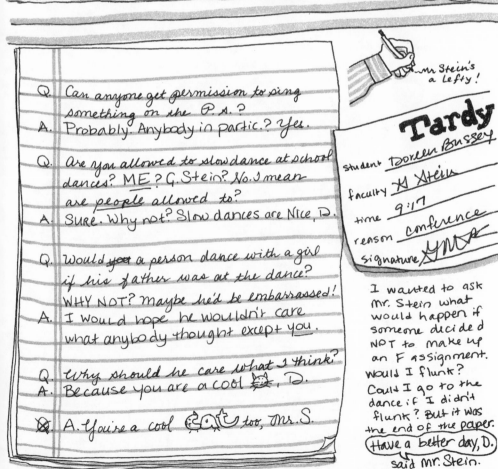

Rats!

Pairs of things mating. That is NOT what I want to think about but that is what's on the schedule of good old Mr. Travis and science class.

I vant to be alone.

← me as a rat

I didn't want to think about *mating* or pairings or pairs or twos or 2's.

2 many 2s 2 think of 2day !

Mom + Dad	Dodo + Marco	Staci + Sven	marco's Dad + Farkle Farley	Cootie + Waldo
= 2	= 2	= 2	= 2	= 2

(And then there is Momo who seems to be just me 1 alone.)

(But also those other fifth-graders I saw this morning, in their ODD numbers:

1

3

There must be some way to get even....

Just when I think we're going all MATHEMATICAL, Mr. Travis puts a Punnett Square up on the board and lets me fill it in.

I am one cool rat cha-cha.

He sez C means black and c means white.
(That's what he sez.)

How do a black rat + another black rat have a white rat child?

R A T L O V E

MOM RAT
C|c → C=black

DAD RAT C=black

	black CC	Cc black
	black cC	cc white

SECRET THOUGHT

maybe Marco + I will BOTH have a white father and a black stepmother. Yes mom is stepmom. At least she's not a FARKLE!

Is it sketchy to be the white rat of the family? (like the black sheep?)

Even if I wasn't in the mood for 2, drawing rats and writing charts and figuring out what goes in the spaces is good for my particular brain.

When the period ended, the bell rang, but Mr. Travis yelled, "Whoa, Nellie!" and proclaimed, "Something to think about:"

CORNELL UNIVERSITY did a study of pigeon flocks and found out the reason there are different MORPHS (different looks) for pigeons = white, grey, brown, etc.: because the pigeons pick pigeons that look like themselves to mate with. Do you think rats do this? And what about people? FOOD 4 THOUGHT

He gave us a copy to write about for homework.

On my way to MS. Sparkle Farkle Farley's lovely social studies class, I felt the urge to stir something up.

Ms. Farley? Can I ask your opinion on this, since you're a SOCIAL STUDIES EXPERT? Do you think it's good for our SPECIES if we mate with people who are just like us or NOT LIKE US? Rich + poor? old + young? Mean + nice?

Well, YOU'RE the one who said WE'RE all the Same under our FUR, Doreen.

Oh, and here's my book. I whispered this. Yes, she makes me put my book on her desk at the beginning of class so I won't be tempted to DOODLE. Witch.

oh, look! Another lefty!

But "Whoa, Nellie!" all over again, because did you NOTICE she remembered my political cartoon??

I said, "You remembered my political cartoon, Ms. Farley!"

"YES," she said in big, hard-edged block letters.

"How could I forget it? Doreen, are you aware that you failed that essay NOT because it included a so-called political cartoon, but because you did not support your opinion with one single fact or quotation or resource? And it was a very weak cartoon and nothing to do with politics."

I said, So?

Ms. Farley has "cat-eye" glasses, and it's true: sometimes Sven glares at me just like she does. But is it the glasses? Or is it her eyes?

Or is it just HER?

So? So? So is all you have to say, Doodlebug?

She does not say Doodlebug in a nice way at all. She says it like she thinks it's a dumb name. But then,

You draw very well. Everybody notices it.

"Thanks," I whispered. Because she wasn't finished.

But you can't JUST draw. You can't draw instead of doing an assignment. Not in MY class.

"I'm a VISUAL LEARNER," I protested.

And I'm a great swimmer! But that's not the best way to get to school!

I resisted saying swimming would be the best way if MS. Farley was a fish. Other people were in the classroom now, the bell was going to ring, and this conversation wasn't going where I wanted it to.

Ms. Farley leaned closer to me and fixed me with her cat eyes.

I have VISION, too, and this is what I see. You'd rather DOODLE than anything else. And you've fooled some people around here with it. But I think you're too intelligent for that. The gears in your head are always turning, but you have more ideas than you're letting on. So redo that essay, and put your whole brain into it, not just those pictures in your head! Or forget the April Fool Hop! Now, take a seat.

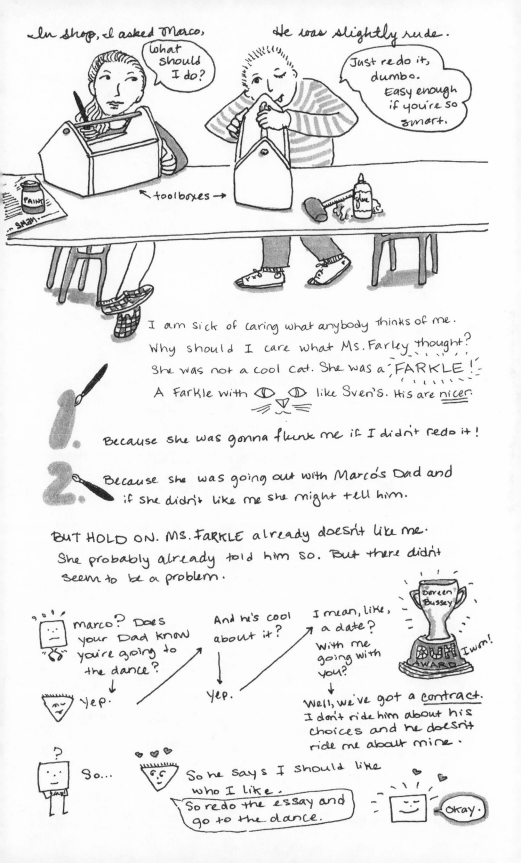

But also

3 Ms. Farkle Farley said I was smart.

Has anyone ever told you you were smart?

It makes you drop paintbrushes and spill paint.

It makes you blush, but you are not really embarrassed.

It blows your socks off:

whoosh!

What it does NOT make you do is want to prove them wrong. You do NOT want to show them your dumbness, even if you have enough to win a nice big trophy for it.

oh,... d...r.....a....g! I can see I'm going to have to redo the essay NOW, that is by Friday, in the middle of moving, worrying about my family, and getting ready for the dance.

Marco? Can I ask you something about your parents?

Yeah.
(But his shoulders went up to his ears.)

How did you know they were really in trouble?

Oh, you'll KNOW.
(He couldn't look at me.)

Did your Dad ever cry about your Mom?

Not that I ever saw. He was so mad. I was the one that cried. I was just 8 and she left me behind. Anything ELSE, Dodo?

(But I couldn't tell Marco it was because Dad didn't have the art job he wanted, when Marco's Dad was successful.)

The bell rang.

Marco and I put our toolboxes away in our shop cubbies and walked down the hall. Marco said,

> I never told anyone that before. It's very **private**.

> Momo's and my mother — our REAL mother — left when I was three and she was one. I think I remember a lot of things but I pretend to forget them ALL. **Why should I even want to** remember _her_? My mom now is my _real_ REAL mom. Don't tell anyone, okay, Magic Marco?

I did not say (it was _too_ **private**):

• • • what happens if my Dad decides to leave? (for good, I mean, not just to L.A. for the U-Haul.)

• • Do I have to go with him because he's the real parent?

• Why is my Dad so upset because Mom's underwear (ad) went national?

I was no closer to an answer (or answer_s_) when we got to lunch. But one thing became extremely obvious:

People were being mean to Momo.

That's why she was at our table again: she wasn't too cool for fifth grade; she was too _uncool_.

Those **3** girls went past our table giggling.

> Hey, Miss Maureen Bussey! Those are some 'O Beautiful' Twinkies you're making there!

And then the most amazing thing happened: The little fifth grade twerps saw Elizabeth. She had frozen with her mouth wide open, right in the middle of taking a bite of her tuna wrap. She st_a_red. They stopped.

She smiled. They went AWAY. (yay.)

Right away another thing became extremely obvious.

Just half a Twinkie wasn't gonna be enough today.

Hey, Mo, I'll buy if you'll fly.

Momo made another Twinkie run while Marco, Cootie, and I put our heads together.

Who are those pea-pickers?

Little fifth-grade choir chicks who never got a Solo and never sang on the P.A. and never WILL!

mean
hateful
nasty
gnarly
immature
jerky
idiotic

Definitely a case of the big green monster. Well, you shut THEM up, Cootie.

OH!

I realized: those girls were jealous.
(And, in the back of my mind, I began to realize that Dad was jealous of Mom.)
(But I had a job to do here.)

"Cootie!" I said. "You know how you said Michael Jackson was Waldo's karaoke specialty?

Her eyes lit up just like mine.

Thriller!" she said. "You know, the one where the monsters are rising from the grave and then they all begin to moonwalk—"

"Does he have a karaoke machine?" I interrupted.

"Why are you bringing this up now?" asked Marco.

"Because we're going to fix things for Momo," I said.

I'm IN.

but how?

Definitely. Bless their hearts.

I said, "I need you both or it won't happen. Marco, I need you to work your magic on Ms. Farley. And Elizabeth Cootie Catcher, I need—"

"A balloon? A crane? A plane?"

"A TRICK . . . . ➤ She smiled.

That afternoon, we drove a very long way to IKEA and came back loaded.

We bought shelves and stools and curtains and rugs and garbage cans and couch pillows and a lamp and batteries and a dish drain and a doormat and lightbulbs and plants and meatballs.

Just GET them!

$5!

but...

We spent $647.85 and yet Mom went and had a **dilemma** about a string of five light-up birds that only cost $5.

"Why wouldn't you get them if you like them?" asked Momo.

"It's just, I'm not sure it's the right thing," said Mom. She was even whining a little.

"Mother," I said, all bossy. "For $5 you can afford to make a mistake."

"I'm not sure," Mom whined. She wouldn't put them in her bag, she walked away. So I put them in one of Momo's bags and we put them under something as we were paying and she never even saw them until we were back at the new little house unpacking the stuff.

Her eyes filled up and she pressed the tip of each index finger to each eye to stop herself. She said, in a deep, husky voice, "BIRDS FLY TO THE STARS, I GUESS." She said it was a line from the movie MOONSTRUCK. "This old grumpy man says it, to be romantic to his lady." So it WAS about Dad. Oh.

SKINA

The little house was not empty when we got there.
Inside the front door we saw:

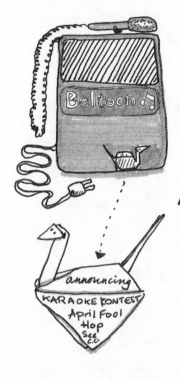

It's from the Cootie Catcher!

Merciful Heavens, what now?

A KARAOKE MACHINE? Hot diggety!!!

It was a paper crane like the ones Cootie Catcher had folded and used to get people to petition to let Momo in the choir when we first came to our school. Then, all Momo cared about was getting to sing in the choir. At our old school she had her three best friends AND she never had to try out for choir. Everybody just knew her and her voice and loved her and loved it. Now it looked like all the stuff she had had to do to get into choir (and what Cootie did, too) had made everybody NOT like her.

Because here is what happened when she saw the crane:

She plopped right down onto the empty floor and sobbed.

I can't!!!

"But Mo," Mom said. "You love karaoke!"

It would be the worst thing I could possibly do!!!

"Come on," said Mom. "You might even win."

That would be the worst thing that could possibly happen!

"Why?" asked Mom. I stayed out of it.

Because they already hate me and then they'd hate me even MORE!

"Who?" asked Mom.

The coolest girls in the WORLD!!

Well, then I was shocked speechless.

Mom waited until Momo calmed down a little, then asked,

"Who are these coolest girls in the world?"

"Coconlilynsasha!" said Momo.

"Who?" I said. But Elizabeth had told me already.

coco. lily. sasha.

MOMO SAID:

coco. She's really skinny and strong and she does gymnastics and she speaks Chinese and she has a saltwater aquarium in her bedroom. Her really old grandmother shares the bedroom with her and in the morning they tell each other their dreams and one time her grandma had this crazy frog dream...

lily. She's really fancy and lacy and her room's all shabby chic from Target and she brings sushi she made HERSELF for lunch. And in the summer she goes to East Texas to see her family and she has a really good fake Texas accent and...

sasha. She has a twin brother in the other fifth grade and he's really short and weird but she's tall and funny. She knows 59,000 knock-knock jokes and she even has a web site of them and she has a dog named Beagle and she's really good at video games and she...

"enough!!" I said. "STOP!"

I had to say it every time. Momo wanted these girls for friends BAD. But Mom said,

"They sound great, Momo."

"They ARE."

"They sound like people you'd really get along with."

"Well, they DON'T. I don't."

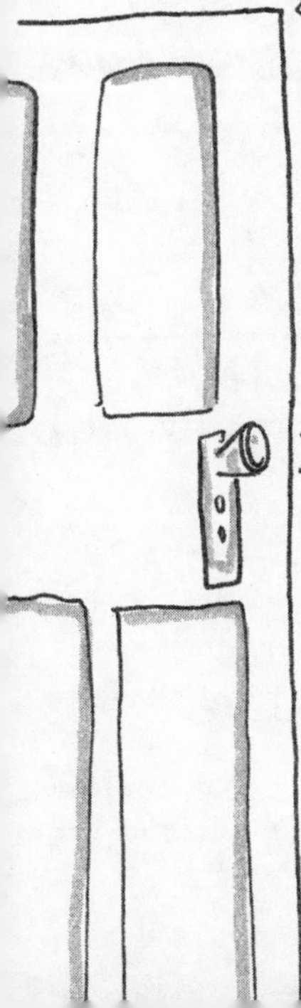

knock knock said our new door.

"Who's there?" called Mom.

"Me!" said an unmistakable voice. "The famous COOTIE CATCHER with her soon-to-be famous backup singers, the COOTIE-ETTES: coconlilynsasha!"

And me.

Yes, it's Waldo and his amazingly antique collection of karaoke songs.

Momo and I were Speechless so Mom said, "How antique?"

In answer, Elizabeth popped in a tape and began to sing

If you change your mind I'm the first in line....

we all said, "ABBA?"
Because that was the golden oldie that insane girl had picked.

Mom said, "This must be the day for the Swedish influence."

Everyone was silent and VERY awkward. mom said, "You know, because ABBA is a Swedish musical group and we have just come back from IKEA, which is a Swedish store, and —"

"Mom!" I whispered and gave her the giant eyes and she said, "Now, very soon we have to get home to that Swedish cat, Sven, so if you'll all pardon me, I'll go hang up some curtains."

go away please please dear mommy

Okay, now, Miss Maureen Bussey, can I count on you and the Cootie-ettes for some quality backup?

And before anyone could QUIBBLE or QUESTION, Waldo hit PLAY and Momo led the Cootie-ettes while Elizabeth the Cootie sang lead.

Take a chance, Take a chance, Take a chance

Pssst! Elizabeth!

You don't expect us to...

Is Maureen gonna be a Cootie-ette?

You know, fifth-graders, there's a reason I asked you to sing backup for me.

WHAT?

People only call me Maureen to be formal. I'm momo.

It's because they're good singers, right? Isn't that what you told me? Cootie?

Elizabeth gave me a look. We hadn't talked about THIS PART. But she didn't miss a trick. She said, "Yep. And I want all you girls to pick out a song to **Solo** with in the karaoke contest."

MOMO the rock star bounced over to Waldo and started going through his music. "You can download Karaoke songs, if anybody wants," he suggested. Coco, Lily, and Sasha said, "**Solos**?" I could see they had just become very nervous suddenly. THE REST OF US SIMPLY LET THEM DEAL WITH IT FOR A MOMENT. AND THEN I GOT AN INCREDIBLY LARGE brain wave.

"Waldo," I said. "Where's Waldo? Don't you need to rehearse your song? There are plenty of zombies here."

"**Dodo!**" whispered Momo, just as I'd expected. Her face was pink and it just got redder as Waldo began to **MOONWALK** and everyone else but her joined in.

Here is a fact of my life: I like to dance but I don't know—or care—what it looks like. I am sloppy and shambling and I can't do steps. Here is a fact of Momo's life: she HATES to dance because she can't. Especially in front of people. Why?

BECAUSE she's uncoordinated...

Sasha put Momo's shoe back on for her.

Lily said, "At least you can sing, Maureen."

Coco helped her up from where I'd left her on the floor.

Momo said, "It's MOMO. It means 'peach' in Japanese. Don't call me Maureen unless I'm dead and it's my funeral or we're onstage and you're introducing me."

Lily said, "Well, you sure won't make it onstage for dancing."
Coco said, "So Momo, is your elbow busted?"

Cootie-Catcher whispered, "Not if it's on her microphone arm!" But none of the fifth grade girls heard.

Sasha said, "You can be a Cootie-ette, too, okay?"

And Momo, humble for once in her life, said, "SURE."

In the kitchen (where we were hiding), Waldo high-fived Cootie, who high-fived me, and I high-fived Mom.

(To myself I wondered, "What's gonna happen when Momo starts showing off?" Because where singing is involved, it's bound to happen.)

Okay. Solos, anyone?

"I dibs R.E.S.P.E.C.T.," said Momo.

"Hey!" I said. "That has a part I can sing: sock it to me sock it to me sock it to me."

"You're going to let HER sing with you?" asked Coco.
(Ha! Being the villainous sister was o.k. with me.)

"Sorry, gang. I'm going to have to ask you to break it up."

"We had packing to do tonight, not to mention homework and feeding Sven."

"See you tomorrow,"

everybody said.

Mom had put out almost all of the IKEA stuff. She had hung the curtains in all the windows, found places for plants on the counters and windowsills, set up the lamp in the living room, thrown throw rugs around, put the dish drain by the sink and the garbage cans in the kitchen and bathroom. But the bird lights were still in the box, tucked behind a plant on a counter. Hmmm. I grabbed the cell phone. *1

DAD? Where are you?

The connection was rotten but I could hear him saying he was staying in Redondo Beach with Uncle Jackson. "It's warm here, Dodo! Wish you were here!"

So did I. Didn't I? Not really.

"Is that Dad?" Yelled Momo.

"Tell him about the karaoke."

"Is that Dad? Did he CALL?"

Mom could tell from my face that he hadn't.

"Tell him I'm singing ARETHA in the karaoke contest!" yelled Momo.

I did. I said we'd gone to IKEA and got tons of stuff and that Mom was getting all set up and we couldn't wait for the U-Haul to get here with the boxes and beds and all. "WHAT?" said Dad. Then he said he and Uncle Jackson were getting the U-Haul tomorrow. He didn't say he couldn't wait to get here with the boxes and beds. And he didn't ask to talk to Mom. I hung up. We went home to Sven.

SHARKS! Fish. Water. Diving. Even some <u>drips.</u>*

* Are you paying attention, Cootie?  Barely.

Something was strange when we got back to the apartment.

"Did we leave the lights on?" asked Mom. But we never do. We are very concerned about wasting energy and leaving the lights on all day is not a very GREEN thing to do.

There was a little tiny part of me that wished that it was Dad, even though he had just told me he was in Redondo! That would be a good trick, but there was no U-Haul.

It was Staci! home early all the way from Japan!

Yoo-hoo, Svenny! Did you turn the lights on?

momo was in a loud and happy mood which was a nice change, apart from the racket. "Shush!" said Mom.

Welcome back!

Wave hi, Sven!

I made it onto an earlier flight and HERE I AM!

Welcome home!

And we all waved back to Sven.

purrrrrr It was weird. We were saying Welcome Home to Staci, except it felt like OUR home, except it was really HER home that we'd been BORROWING of course. And OUR real home was now going to be in the sweet little house, except that wasn't home yet. And it didn't feel like Dad was there yet.

And if we needed further proof of weirdness, there was the Swedish kitty SVEN, who had always been a hidey-cat, a scaredy-cat, and very standoffish and under-the-beddish, purring in Staci's arms and letting her wave his paw like a Chinese beckoning cat puppet!

oh Sven, did you hate us all along and just want her?

Who could blame Sven for wanting Staci? She was...

cool

Momo and I had watched the Mouth the Almighty cartoon that she **made** and **left for us** along with **Sven** himself and her cozy apartment that felt like it was in a tree.

(you couldn't help being a fan of such a cool person.)

warm with her big smile, bright eyes, friendly (? Sven?) waving cat, and her jolly welcome like we were HER family.

Seriously! Little candy dolls! How cute are they?

(She even brought us Japanese candy, although she hadn't even met Momo and me since we were tiny and had only met Mom at Mom and Dad's wedding. Staci had been one of Dad's ushers even though she is female.)

Aunt Wendy (Dad's sister)   Aunt Wanda (mom's sister)   Minnie (mom's friend)   Aunt Iris (mom's sister)   Mom   Dad   momo me   Uncle Jackson (Dad's brother)   Staci John (Dad's friends)   Uncle Hank (mom's brother)

It also crossed my mind and was later confirmed by (1) Elizabeth (2) Marco and (3) Waldo (but never even mentioned to Momo, who was freaked out enough, but not as freaked out as I was about Mom and Dad) that Staci might also be seen by Dad as

hot with her bouncy hair, curvy curves, fabulous eye-popping flowered dress, funny laugh, and so on.

THAT NIGHT momo and I lay talking in the half-dark of the living room (lit by the star lights and the star light and the city lights and Momo was all happy and excited about the karaoke Kontest and all hopeful that she and CoconLilynSasha were going to become a big jolly foursome like her L.A. friends had been. She finally conked out and I didn't.

Mom and Staci

sat in the kitchen and talked and it wasn't long before they got off the subjects of JAPAN and tighty-whiteys and got onto the subject of **DAD**. They didn't know each other very well, but they both knew Mr. Warren G.* Bussey.

"He doesn't have a very healthy ego about his art, our Warn," said Staci.

"our"? Oh yeah, I remember she calls him Warn, from art school days. What's an ego?

"No," said Mom. "He's really hurting now. He had such high hopes for this job and now he's just being a manager and he feels like nobody appreciates his skills there- he IS a good manager!"

"YES, he would be," interrupted Staci.

How does she know? I remember now how Dad used to talk to Staci on the phone all the time when we lived in L.A. and how she was the one who helped him get the S.F. job back in the days when I was screwing up in school and getting expelled.

* stands for Gordon a cool middle name...

Gordon

...because you can write it right-side up and upside down all at once. Dad showed me how. His father, also with the middle name Gordon, showed him. A good name for an ARTIST. If I have a son maybe he'll be a Gordon, too.

Eyeball Industry sounds like a cool place to work. Thanks, Stace.

"He's not getting to do anything creative now."

"For Warn that's devastating," said Staci. She knew.

STILL Staci was _Dad's_ friend. Otherwise - say if it was Mom's sister Iris or her best friend Minnie, Mom might have said... **AND HE'S BRINGING THE STUFF IN THE U-HAUL BUT I'M NOT SURE HE'LL BE HAPPY HERE.** (Doesn't matter: I can still hear it.)

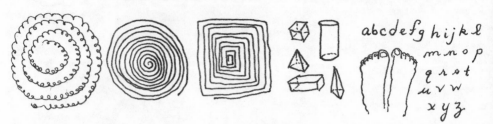

For the longest time that night I sat and drew NOTHING. I did the Curly Spiral and the Smooth Spiral and the Square Spiral. I did the Solid Shapes with their Invisible Bottoms. I wrote the alphabet in pre-cursive (what cursive letters look like before you connect them together). I drew my feet. I am a worried

I thought, "I should be happy now." But I wasn't.

I thought, "There are lots of reasons to be happy." Yes, there really were.

🏠 Cute sweet cozy little house.   CLSA Cootie-ettes.

🩲 Tighty Whitey.   ▽ Magic Marco.   ⊞ Cootie herself.

Even Sven was happy, purring under the bed.

HEY! What are you doing up? Shh, don't wake your Mom and Momo. Just whisper! What are you thinking of with a deep sharky doodle?

I glanced at my doodlebook.

Yup, that's a deep sharky doodle all right!

Are you sinking? Are you surrounded? Not to go all **psychological** on you!

I was trying to seem cheery but truthfully I felt weary.

"**What I'm doing here is rising**", I said.

"How can you tell?" asked Staci.

"See the drips?" I asked.   "OH, GOOD," said Staci.

She sat down and sighed. Traitor Sven padded out from under me and said, "mrrrrout?" to Staci. Thump Thump. She patted the chair next to her leg and he jumped into her lap.

"Wow, Sven," I said.

Staci said, "Imagine being Sven and having me just not come home one night. Then the door opens and four strange people come in and stay and stay and stay."

How could I help it?

I sniffed back my tears.

"Oh, man!" said Staci.

"I'm sorry, Dodo! I'm so thankful to you all! Sven is so calm and open! I can tell you made him feel safe!"

"We love him," I said.

Staci looked out the window. "It's weird that it's dark. It doesn't feel like night. I guess I'm still on Tokyo time."

"I always forget about it being a different time in other places," I said. "I never think anywhere is really real except where I am."

"Like L.A.?" said Staci. "It's all still there. But you all have made a new life here, it sounds like."

I hope so.

You don't know so? Is it because of your dad?

← She knows!

And under the safety of night and with Sven all glad and purring and because I didn't really know Staci and because I knew she was really Dad's friend, I managed to spit out:

He has been e-mailing me about what STARS you and Momo are.

Things are good here for all of us but Dad. I think it makes him feel left out and lonely! I'm afraid he might go—

Then I did stop. It felt like a sleepwalking conversation, like Mom (and Dad) wouldn't know, in the morning, that I'd had this whole adventure without them. But Staci KNEW. STACI just closed her eyes and rocked Sven 'til I fell asleep.

In the morning Staci made us a breakfast feast.

I have a new friend at school named Coco.

She went out before we got up, to buy coffee beans and sourdough rolls at some place in the neighborhood we've never heard of called Victoria's. We wish we'd known about it all right!

She made coffee for her and Mom and cocoa for Momo and me.

I asked, "What was Dad like in college? What was he into? What is his favorite art that you ever saw him do?"

Staci said, "My **favorite** of **all**? Okay, hmm. Top THREE:

1. Once for showcase he made a whole living room out of old thrown-out furniture and painted messages all over it, like on the TV it said "Rot your brain here" and on the couch it said **MELT** in letters made out of cheesey orange.

2. He made a life-size self-portrait and took it to a shooting gallery on the Santa Monica pier and got them to let him shoot holes in it."

"**CRIPES**," said Momo. Mom just listened, and I wondered if she knew all this. It was Mabel who had gone to art school with Staci and Dad, not Mom. Mabel, our so-called Real Mom. "What else?" I said.

3. The Giant Head of the 20th Century, American. It was made out of TV antennas and telephone and computer parts and craziness, all coming out of a head like Superman's. Junk food, sports, the rockets going to the moon — This poor guy had it all coming out of his brains!

It was a great sculpture! It won the big old SENIOR PRIZE! We all thought he was a genius. And it sold for a pile."

"I wish I'd seen it."

"When we were married he made me sculptures of the girls all made out of scrap hardware— nuts and bolts and things— so I wouldn't think it was so complicated taking care of little girls!"

"Yeah, he's always been really talented."

"What has he been working on lately?"

"WORK," said Momo.

I asked, "where'd he get all the garbage stuff from?"

Dumpster Diving!

said Staci and mom.

"Can I call Dad?" I asked. Neither Mom nor Staci had.

"Where are you now?" I asked Dad. Mom and Staci pretended they weren't watching me, but they could hear. Nothing much was new with Dad. He and Uncle Jackson were going to get the U-haul this morning and start filling it up. "I've been hearing how you were a Dumpster Diver!" I said. "Back in the art days!"

"Yeah, that is some ancient history all right!"

"Why'd you stop?" I asked. "No good garbage in the 21st century?"

Mom didn't try to hide her eavesdropping when I hung up. "what was his answer to the stopping question?" she asked. "He said, 'You can't eat scenery, Dodo.'" (I didn't say that I didn't get it!)

Mom explained, "He means he needs a steady income."

I said,

"I need to go to school. MOVE IT, SLO-MO MOMO!"

"Yeah, yeah."

Momo & I ran around grabbing our stuff. We were late. And as I ran and grabbed, it occurred to me that I had not given one single thought to Farkle Farley and her essay.

As we left we heard Staci say,

"Warn just wants to be a good father."

"I know." said Momo sadly.

Dad used to take me and Mo mo to the bumper cars on the pier at Santa Monica.

BOOM! BOOM! BOOM! EEK! me

Everyone crashing into everyone else. That's how school felt when we got there this morning. YIKES!

First, that little short kid in the bow tie latched onto Momo. She walked faster. He caught up.

It's about the April Fool Hop, Maureen! WAIT!

She did not wait. I did not see what her problem was.

It's about the Karaoke Kontest! Hang on a sec!

Nice one, momo!

Momo said, "Ask my sister!" And took off for homeroom.

May I help you?

I wanta sing "We are the Champions."

Good Gosh George Washington, what next?

I'll put you on the list. What's yer name?

He wears a bow tie on an elastic over a GIANTS tee shirt. Really, truly.

His name is **Franky**. Franky Petrov. He's **Sasha's** twin brother! In a classic Dododuh moment, I say, "You don't look anything like Sasha." He says brightly, "THANKS for the info!" After I've written Franky Petrov in my doodlebook, I escape. And that's when I see that **Elizabeth**, the **COOTIE CATCHER**, also known as Colleen Callahan has struck again with her paper publicity.

Her Karaoke fish swimming along.

All down the hall I see her origami advertisements. And at the end of the hall I see the pink cheeks of

The **Trouble** is, there isn't going to be any karaoke kontest if Ms. Farley has anything to say about it! And it's mainly your fault but I also blame my dad and her....

"This might be love," said Magic Marko.

And right there in homeroom where I was sitting at my desk with THAT NOTE from the Social Studies department in my hand, Marco took his red prismacolor pen out of his back pocket and drew on my hand. "Think about it!" he said. "Ms. Farley is not going away. She has a MAD CRUSH on my dad and he says he is SMITTEN."

"Meaning...?"

"Hit by love," said Marco.

And then I said a really mean thing and I don't begin to know why I would act that way but

"Teachers don't make much money," I said.

"And your dad makes a decent **buck**. He's rich!"

The bell rang. We left homeroom and headed for our first classes. Marco had to say guten tag to German, and I had to say ¿que pasa? to Spanish. Without really thinking, I unfolded my note and read it.

Marco was still fixated on his father. He said, "He says she has a beautiful heart."

I didn't even glance at the ♡ on my hand

I just went ahead and said the meanest thing ever:

"It's just that she's a teacher," I said. "And she doesn't have any money. So..."

Marco's face grew deep pink, then red, then dark red.

He pointed upstairs, toward Ms. Farley's room.

I said, "I don't know."

SOCIAL STUDIES DEPARTMENT

Student **Doreen D. Bussey**
is in danger of failing

Course **Western Civilization 2**

Teacher **Farley**

effective date **April 2**

comments **Student received F on major assignment of grading period and has not made up the credit**

student signature **X**

He pointed at the note

You know you have to sign it and take it to her.

He pointed at me

Are you gonna redo your essay, or NOT???

So after being LATE to homeroom, I was LATE to Spanish. I had missed the part of class I like best, when Señor Ramos says, "Hola, clase." (Hello, class) Then we all answer, "¡Hola, Señorrr RRRRRamos!" It is a test of how well you can roll your Rs. Naturally with a name like Ramos, Señor Ramos loves a good R-roll. I work on this. So when I entered, he let out a good loud, "Hola, Dorrrinda." I did my best with his R. Then I sat down next to Elizabeth, opened my book, and showed her Franky's name and song.

We are going to have to put a limit on this or there won't be any time to dance!

And Waldo WON'T like that.

I wrote her a note: There's limits on it all right. Marco says Ms. F won't let us do it at all!

Why? Didn't you rewrite your paper? You'd better or else.

or else what?

Listen Doodle, Waldo has gone to all that trouble of borrowing his cousin's karioki machine and you can't mess this up for me. If you don't it might just be the greatest night of my life so far. He held my hand last night after you went home and I swear I really love

I ... my own problems and it's not my fault if things don't work out for everybody in the whole world!

Nice attitude. Enjoy your Solitude.

Get lost!

In my sketchbook I began to make a list of everyone who thought I was an idiot.

1 Ms. Farley ←
2 Mr. Duffy
3 probably Marco's Dad, thanks to
4 definitely Marco
5 mr. Stein is going to when I don't even show up at the hop.
6 my parents are going to when I get an F in soc. stud.
7
8 momo is going to when there's no Karaoke Kontest. Plus C, L, S.
9, 10, 11
+ Elizabeth- now, in the future and maybe FOREVER!
12

7. YES MAYBE DIE COULD BE, WHO KNOWS

I develop a few new theories.

When classes changed and we left Spanish, all I saw was the back of Cootie Catcher as she walked away. I've got to say, she looked more worried than mad.

That's because it was Waldo she cared about. Not me. (Not Marco either.) If she didn't have me to go to the April Fool Hop, she might not be allowed to go. Not with just Waldo.

So Franky's in the Karaoke thing now too!

Momo went by with Sasha and saw Cootie and me not walking together. She gave me a little wave.

I hauled my tired body all the way to the 3rd floor and science. And as soon as I sat down—right on time!—Mr. Travis commanded us,

"So! EVERYBODY DROP TO THE DESK AND GIVE ME 5 THEORIES!"

Jordan Jamirez plays football too much. He said

Is that like five pushups, Mr. T?

"No, Sirree," said Mr. Travis. "A theory is a statement or idea that needs to be supported with evidence to be proved. Such as... what would be a theory that has to do with the nature-nurture question?" He looked around and said,

BAA!

NATURE THEORY: A sheep behaves like a sheep because it has sheep genes that tell it to.

NURTURE THEORY: A sheep just acts like all the other sheep because it has learned sheep behavior from them.

BAA!

"Doreen Doodlebug Bussey? How does the nature-nurture question lead to theories about sheep behavior?"

← Here is my brilliant answer, may it please his royal highness.

"Fine. Thank you for the sheep pictures also. Theories, anyone? Doreen, you only owe me three more."

3. When you're born you don't know anything.

4. Eggs came first, from dinosaurs, and eventually dinosaurs evolved into chickens.

5. San Franciscans are tougher than people in other cities because they have to walk up so many hills all the time.

At first when I had to write a theory it was the only one I could think of. I wrote #3. #4 took me a long time to think of. I thought I was all out of ideas and I was sure glad I had to write three, not five. But by the time I finished with #5 I thought I could probably write five more.

No problemo:

6. If you never spoke Spanish you would not ever need to roll your Rs.

7. So what if you know paper tricks, you shouldn't just use people to get what you want.

8. If you eat Pop Rocks and drink Coke your ♡ will stop. (my heart is BLACK, I thought. Marco's red heart was still there.)

9. 5th-graders and 7th-graders should stick to their own kind.

10. Some teachers ~~forget~~ totally forget completely what it's like to have to learn.

"Ms. Bussey?" said Mr. Travis. "It's all happening UP HERE now." He pointed at his face. He asked, "What happens to a theory that isn't ever completely proved?" I had had enough of his attention. And, even if he was nice about it, I HATED when teachers said stuff that reminded me that I had borderline A**ttention**! D**eficit**! D**isorder**! and everyone else in the place

Jordan Jamirez, (who was feeling a little disorderly himself today) said, (get this, people!) (Dodo doesn't have enough of something and it makes her disorderly!)

"It dies?"

Hmm. The stop sign of life for unproven theories?? [STOP]

No, you crazy numbskull. It hangs around FOREVER making people wonder! It's a big What if?

Off I went to Farkleland.

I got your note, Ms. Farley.

Here it is, back to you.

No, I didn't sign it. That would be like accepting an F. I can't.

I'm not an F sort of person.

"W E L L," she said.

"Ms. Farley!" I interrupted. "Did you ever notice? When you fold your hands, you cross your left thumb over your right, not the other way around!"

She looked down at her hands. I was already looking at them and (while trying to read the note about the April Fool Hop under her left wrist) noticed how tightly she was clenching her hands. "So?" she said.

"It's special," I said. "It's recessive. Most people do it differently from you. It's genetic!"

Ms. Farley said something then that my Dad says at times:

"Why am I NOT surprised?" She didn't smile.

"Ms. Farley," I said. "Did you ever get an F?"

For the first time today I looked up from her desk at her eyes. "YES," she said in big 3-D block letters.

THE BELL RANG for the start of class. I sat down and typed out (imaginarily) more theories. Ms. Farley seemed

So perfect — kind of a pain!

pretty! punctual! precise! polished! polite (mostly)! professorial! (like a professor) prepared!

WAS IT POSSIBLE THAT IN SCHOOL SHE HAD POSSIBLY BEEN A punk? like me?

I ate my lunch alone.

But first, I drew it all. Until...

Sourdough roll from Victoria's

Granny Smith apple

Edam cheese (in a baggie)

Two whole Twinkies

water

Why, if it isn't the Doodlebug!

It was MS. Wu, our favorite principal. That is what she tells us to call her. But to be honest I think I would anyway. Ms. Wu has rocked my world on more than one occasion. And now she positively looks like an angel. Before I even get the word HELLO out of my mouth she jumps right into my life and says,

I've never seen darling Mr. Stein so excited!

And maybe it's because I've been hanging around with the Cootie Catcher, but suddenly I got a tricky idea.

Yeah, he can't wait for the big Karaoke Kontest!

I gave Ms. Wu one of my Twinkies and I told her what was going on with Momo.

THEORY:
Please don't think I was being a traitor to Momo! Ms. Wu is her friend and adores her. I was trying to get Ms. Wu on my side by showing her how Momo needed a little Karaoke kindness to help her with the grade 5 kids.

See, Elizabeth Kaur and I realized how some of the 5th grade girls thought Momo was a snob because she sings so well. They were jealous so we figured if we could get them in a Karaoke group with Momo they'd be friends. And it worked! Only if there's no Kontest, there might be a problem, and Ms. Farley told Marco she didn't want to DEAL with karaoke..........

ME BEST. ✶ TODAY'S THEORIES ✶ IF YOU BRING AN UMBRELLA. IT WON'T RAIN ✶ DAD CAN BE A GOOD DAD AND A SCULPTOR ✶ IT'S HARD TO BE FRIENDS (OR MARRIED) IF YOU'RE JEALOUS ✶ MS. FARLEY GOT AN F IN ART ✶ NO. IN GYM ✶ NO. IN SOCIAL STUDS. ✶ SVEN SECRETLY LOVES

ALL THE REST OF THE DAY I WAS ALONE (EXCEPT FOR SVEN.) I was alone with all my thoughts, and theories kept going around in my head like the NEWS ZIPPER in the school cafeteria. ✶ I would have LIKED TO KNOW if Elizabeth would have agreed with my idea of getting Ms. Wu in on the Karaoke Kontest. Or would she think I was a rat?

One thing I knew for sure: when Ms. Wu mentioned the K. K. to Mr. Stein, he would not rat me out. He'd say, "What! You've never heard me sing LAST DANCE?"

✶ I wanted very much to know what Marco thought Ms. Farkle Farley got her F in. And maybe it wasn't just one F!

✶ I wanted to know how Momo was doing, and I wanted to talk to her about my idea for saving Mom and Dad and our NEW life in the NEW little house. But she went to Coco's house to practice with Elizabeth and the Cootie-ettes and I went home alone.

RATS!

✶ when I got home I called Dad on his cell phone. the NEWS was not good. The U-Haul was burning up so that he stopped in Santa Barbara and switched all the stuff to a NEW U-Haul and now he wouldn't get here til midnight!!

For some reason I decided not to even THINK about the essay until Dad got here. (why?) CALIFORNIA S.F. Santa Barbara L.A.

✶ I did my homework until Mom and Staci came home. We went to TARGET, then took the stuff we got to the house. Then we went home to Staci's for takeout Chinese. YUK.

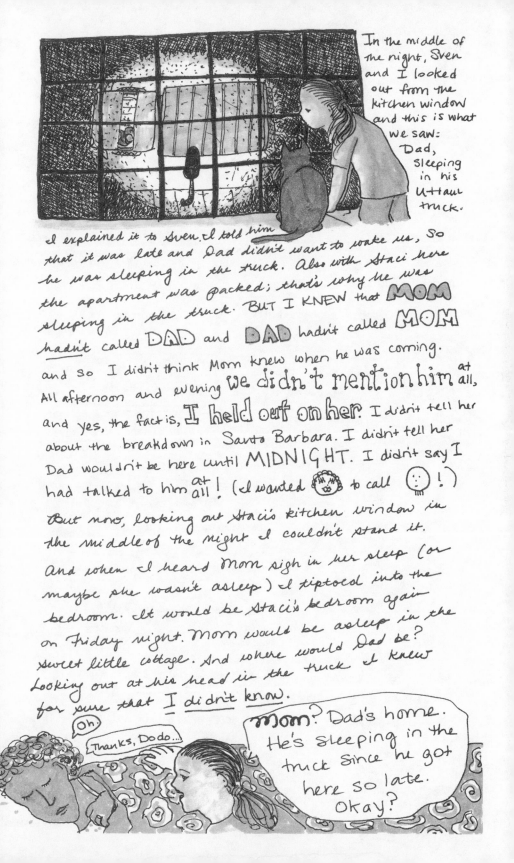

In the middle of the night, Sven and I looked out from the kitchen window and this is what we saw: Dad, sleeping in his U-Haul truck.

I explained it to Sven. I told him that it was late and Dad didn't want to wake us, so he was sleeping in the truck. Also with Staci here the apartment was packed; that's why he was sleeping in the truck. BUT I KNEW that **MOM** hadn't called **DAD** and **DAD** hadn't called **MOM** and so I didn't think Mom knew when he was coming. All afternoon and evening **we didn't mention him** at all, and yes, the fact is, **I held out on her.** I didn't tell her about the breakdown in Santa Barbara. I didn't tell her Dad wouldn't be here until MIDNIGHT. I didn't say I had talked to him at all! (I wanted 🙂 to call 🙂 !) But now, looking out Staci's kitchen window in the middle of the night I couldn't stand it. And when I heard Mom sigh in her sleep (or maybe she wasn't asleep) I tiptoed into the bedroom. It would be Staci's bedroom again on Friday night. Mom would be asleep in the sweet little cottage. And where would Dad be? Looking out at his head in the truck I knew for sure that I didn't know.

Oh. Thanks, Dodo...

Mom? Dad's home. He's sleeping in the truck since he got here so late. Okay?

 **In the morning,** things seemed brighter. Don't they always? Yes, but this was special.

The kitchen seemed crowded: 5 people and a cat! **Sven** sat in his sphinx position, just listening. **Svinx.**

I was feeling quiet, too, and tired, and edgy, and worried.

I had a lot to do, and I didn't know if I could do it.

The one talking was **MOMO** and pretty soon I realized that she was talking **SO MUCH** because the grown-ups were asking her so many questions. They were asking me, too, but Momo was the one answering.

> WHAT'S ALL THIS I HEAR about a karaoke kontest?

The sphinx would be even quieter with a nice mug of cocoa.

> ARE THE COOTIE-ETTES holding another rehearsal today?

> SO WHO ARE THESE GUYS who are going to bust a few Michael Jackson moves at the dance?

> Yep, the one and only Momo will be under the lights again!

> I was NOT born to sing backup, but it's nice to have friends

> SERIOUSLY, do you think Judy Garland's friends thought she was a snot?

> You mean the boyfriends? Marco Polo and Where's Waldo!

snicker snicker tee hee hee

I realized it was easier for Dad, Mom, and Staci to focus on us than to talk among themselves in front of us — and I wondered what would happen when we went to school!

I grumped at Momo, "You sound like one of those twitty 5TH GRADE GIRLS!"

Mom said, "She IS a twitty 5th grade girl!"

"**MOM!**" said Momo. "**JO!**" said Dad.

mom said, "**Move it, girls.** I'm walking you to school

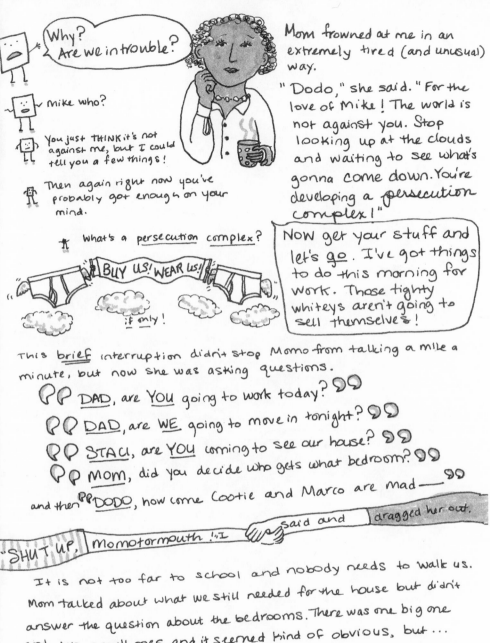

Why? Are we in trouble?

Mike who?

You just THINK it's not against me, but I could tell you a few things!

Then again right now you've probably got enough on your mind.

What's a persecution complex?

BUY US! WEAR US!

if only!

Mom frowned at me in an extremely tired (and unusual) way.

"Dodo," she said. "For the love of Mike! The world is not against you. Stop looking up at the clouds and waiting to see what's gonna come down. You're developing a persecution complex!"

NOW get your stuff and let's go. I've got things to do this morning for work. Those tighty whiteys aren't going to sell themselves!

This brief interruption didn't stop Momo from talking a mile a minute, but now she was asking questions.

DAD, are YOU going to work today?

DAD, are WE going to move in tonight?

STACI, are YOU coming to see our house?

MOM, did you decide who gets what bedroom?

and then DODO, how come Cootie and Marco are mad—

"SHUT UP, Momotormouth!" I said and dragged her out.

It is not too far to school and nobody needs to walk us. Mom talked about what we still needed for the house but didn't answer the question about the bedrooms. There was one big one and two small ones and it seemed kind of obvious, but...

As soon as we got to school, Momo saw CoconLilynSasha and evaporated.

Then Mom said, "You don't need to have a PERSECUTION COMPLEX, Dodo. You're a strong, gifted person, so people are going to ask a lot of you. They're not picking on you, they NEED you. Rise above it! Be your best self!"

She said this in her usual PEP-TALK voice, but her eyes were sad.

"my LIFE felt like it was in pieces" "I had to start putting things together or else!" "So I went to see jolly old" "mr. Stein."

He was in his office in the office outside Ms. Wu's office with the magic P.*A.** system button on his desk.

Doreen Dodo Doodlebug! What can I do you for?

I need to **address the *public, Mr. S.

I had things all written out on a card. Mr. Stein gave it the once-over, then pressed the P.A. button. "**Good morning, students**," he said.

I leaned toward the P.A. machine:

Cootie Catcher productions

with special guest WALDO SINGH announces a once-in-a-lifetime karaoke kontest coming to you at FRIDAY NIGHT'S April Fool Hop. Sign up with Elizabeth Kaur by dismissal TODAY.

I made the O.K. sign to Mr. Stein and he leaned in to give the real, true announcements while I skedaddled to homeroom.

INCOMING!
POW!

Elizabeth had written:

flat balloon:

you wrote it?

I shook my head. NOPE!!

In homeroom

Franky Petrov brought me a new copy of my in danger of failing note. "See me after school today!" Ms. Farley had written across it.

GIANTS

Elizabeth spied over my shoulder and read it. "There had better BE a kontest!" she said.

Franky reminded me a little of the story of Rumpelstiltskin my mom used to read us. It gave me an idea of a deal I could make with Ms. Farley.

The miller's daughter has to guess Rumpelstiltskin's name.

I asked him a question:

You have until the end of the day. Ms. Farley

Señor Ramos greeted me, "Dorinda, tienes una nota."

Señor Ramos, why would somebody flunk Spanish?

printer paper from Ms. Keller

Dear Ms. Farley,
I would like to write you an essay of theories. They are guesses about something. I will support my guesses with facts and observations based on experience and research. There will be quotations from experts. And the essay will come to you piece by piece. When I get the correct theory, the essay will be done. And you will pass me. And I can go to the hop.

I put his answer into my first theory:

I do not theorize that Ms. Farley's F was in Spanish. To fail a foreign language, says Señor Hector Ramos, a student must refuse to memorize or have trouble remembering. Or maybe he just doesn't care enough. Or maybe he never bothers to roll his Rs. Or cuts class. Or cheats.

I got Elizabeth to deliver it. What is it?

Right. Like you thought Cootie wasn't going to read it?!

She laughed! She said she got an A in French and went to Paris as an exchange student in high school. She said to tell you, "Bon chance!" It means, "Good luck!" And she wrote a mean note.

Thanks very much. Cootie Catcher. You can go now!

Social Studies Department
Doreen, It will not be enough to tell me why someone would fail. If your theory is that I have not failed, you will have to show why not. You can't just guess wildly like the girl in Rumpelstilt-

Dear Ms. Farley,
You never forget anything. It's almost like you can't forget. You care about whatever you do, maybe a little too much. And you are conscientious and well-behaved to cut class or cheat. I don't know if rolling Rs is important in French but if it was, then I know that you

I dashed into Ms. Farley's room before science.

Ms. Farley, I know you hate me and Marco drawing, but I don't think you flunked art. The only way you can flunk art is if you cut or don't do any assignments. And, you would do them all even if you stunk. wouldn't you??

At the beginning of social studies I handed Ms. Farley another piece of essay.

Ms. Farley, I bet you didn't get an A in science because I don't think you have a very inquisitive mind, as Mr. Jasper Travis says you need. But you didn't fail because you always follow proper procedure and understand the importance of

I felt a bit rude, but this was SCIENCE!

"Evidence NEEDS TO BE ROCK SOLID," Ms. Farley said. "You may have to apply your Scientific Method and see what experiments show to be sure you really know what you think you know. Okay, Doodlebug? Now sit."

She held out her hand for my doodlebook, and I handed it over.

Did you hear that? ° ° ° I asked myself.

She called me Doodlebug!

DOODLE POWER

And at the end of the class she handed me back my essay pieces. On the back of one she'd written

In fact, I am jealous of your and Marco's art.
I do so have an inquisitive mind.

MAKE SURE you come and see me after school today.

She didn't say WHERE to see her after school. Was this a chance to get Ms. F to think outside the box? OR was I, once again, being a rude dope? Hmmm.

In shop class, the toolboxes were finished. I liked almost everything about my toolbox: I liked the smoothness of the wood I had sanded, the house-shaped ends I had cut, the way the dowel handle fitted tightly into the round joints at the ends.

PERFECT!

(It just needed some doodled decorations.)

"Can I come next time Ms. Farley goes to your house for dinner?"

"She's coming **TONIGHT**. You want to come **TONIGHT**?"

I had a hunch about Marco and about where I could go to make my toolbox even better than perfect before putting some new tools in it and taking it to our new house.

Marco's face was practically pale. He seemed **SO MAD**. But at that moment I was more concerned about the possible **F** than I was about that hop dance. Except right then I found myself wondering:

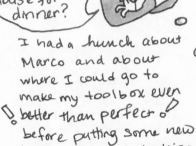

is Marco's hair PRICKLY or soft?

What is my exact problem?

Especially now when Marco is talking all mean as if we are having an **ARGUMENT**?

But if I left it up to Marco to invite me over so I could talk to MS. Farley AFTER SCHOOL TODAY, he might just not, because he was being all pissy.

I asked, "Could we decorate our toolboxes together?"

"Okay," said 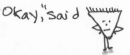 "I just got some new colors."

All day long I asked teachers how to fail their classes.

"Are you going to post this on your Fabulous Page?" asked Ms. Michaels. "How to Fail?" It was a cool idea, actually.

And Ms. Wu had been asking me to post something new.

All day long I sent paragraphs to Ms. Farley about how she had not failed this or that.

All day long she wrote back to tell me the ways I was wrong.

Q No F in gym because the only way to fail gym was to cut or refuse to play? And she was too well-behaved for that?

A Ms. F wrote back, "I'm a good athlete. That's why I went to, participated in, and aced gym."

Q No F in math because she was clearly a logical thinker and also the kind of person who would go to Extra Help if she had trouble with, say, decimals?

A Ms. F wrote back that she was on the math team in school.

Nerd Alert!

Q No F in English because she clearly liked to write, so she must like reading, too. I even asked the school librarian for evidence, and she looked up and said,

"Tell her she's had Harry Potter* Six for much longer than necessary and there are STUDENTS on the reserve list for it!" Speaking of nerd alerts, Ms. Farley was beginning to remind me of a certain TYPE A, frizzy-haired, good student, always has an answer sort of female character in the * Massive Book Heart Attack Fantasy Series itself.

A Ms. Farley said, "You're getting warm" as she passed me in the hallway at dismissal.

I was on my way to pick up my toolbox from shop, so I asked my shop teacher about failing, just in case and to cover all bases.

You know what I just realized? And I will be for at least the Tighty Whitey moon! BUT if Dad hadn't taken his job BUT you just can't be sad back of a cable car

I am a San Franciscan now! next year, thanks to Mom and none of us would have come here at Eyeball Industry. Oh Dad! if you're hanging on to the going up a big hill.

wheee!

PLUS, I have a job to do when I get to Marco's. 2 jobs. No, wait. 3 jobs. Not even! I have 4 jobs. AND, I have to get home soon for our last night with Staci & Sven!

ORT! ORT! you can hear sea lions from Marco's

Riding the elevator to Marco's apartment, I formed a plan. BUT I didn't count on Ms. Farley. She and Marco's dad

must be getting pretty tight.

2107

DODO, you are SO DEAD.

well, well, well. If it isn't Ms. Sparkle Farkle Farley.

I took a deep breath.

Hi, Ms. Farley, are you enjoying the beauteous view?

Doreen, you really must think that I'm SIMPLEMINDED. Of course, "after school" could mean any time from dismissal to midnight, couldn't it, especially to a free-thinking person like you.

I nodded. I walked toward her. I wasn't scared of her. (Marco was. He evaporated, disappearing into another room. what had he and Ms. Farley talked about before I got here?)

Ms. Farley spun her chair toward me, and as she did she took the book off her lap and tucked it under her, the pen tucked inside. Then she acted as if it wasn't there in a way that made me notice it even more. For instance: wasn't that a Prismacolor pen, the sort that gives MAGIC MARCO his name?

"Ms. Farkle," I said, distracted by that pen, "are you sneaking around DOODLING?"

She was going to say it. I could tell. She was leaning toward me to break it to me not-so-gently that I had earned a big fat old grade F in her class of social studies.

"Don't say it!" I said. "You said I had to the end of today to guess what you got an F in. Well today goes on to midnight! You said so yourself!"

When she got a word in edgewise, she didn't sound mad at all. She said in a cool, calm voice,

Here are the theories you've put forward. Listen carefully. NOT Spanish. NOT Art. NOT Science. NOT Shop. NOT gym. NOT Math. NOT English.

NOW, like Rumpelstiltskin, I'm prepared to give you 3 more chances. You have already gone over my head by taking the Karaoke Kontest to Ms. Wu and Mr. Stein, so I no longer have that choice. But an F from me will keep you out of that dance.

So guess thoughtfully.

guess #1:

♪ music? ♫

No, as you will see at that Kontest if you guess correctly.

Social Studies its own self?

No. I'm far too interested in people to fail that subject.

guess #2:

And then she said, "Can I ask your opinion on something, Doreen?" ? ? ? ?

She pulled the book out from under her leg and opened it up.

Then, "What do you think?" my teacher asked.

"Well, what would you do?"

"It's good," I said brightly. I even smiled.

"You get an F for honesty," said MS. Farley.

"Why did you call me Ms. Farkle before? Yes, you slipped.

No air in my lungs. Gasp!

I said, "Because you're kind of Miss Perfect."

"Like Sparkle Farkle?" she said. "I used to think she was really funny."

Just then the living room door opened and Marco's father came in. "Hello, ladies," he said. Marco poked his head out of the kitchen, where apparently he had been hiding. **NEWS FLASH** : Ms. Farley didn't hide her picture from THEM. She left it open and laid it face up right on the table.

"Aw, honey, look what you did!" said Marco's father.

"Doodlebug here thinks it needs work," Ms. Farley said.

➤ "DON'T YOU, Doodlebug?" ◄

I met those eyes. "The colors are a little off, I think," I said. "And my eyes just wander around, because there isn't any center or focus."

Ms. Farley smiled the most
gorgeous
big
smile.

And when I saw that smile I got a brilliant idea.
I remembered every report card I'd ever gotten.
And I thought of a grade I realized I
hadn't worried about enough at all
when I'd been worrying about
this very next report card.
And I realized that
of all people
the perfect-seeming
Sparkle Farkle
Farley knew
all about it.

guess #3:

quality report card of long ago

	attendance	attitude	effort
Davis, K.			
Dwight, D.	A	B	
Farley, K.	B	F	
Geiger, C.	B	G	
Hayes, F.	G	A	

"Miss Farley," I said. "Did you get an F for attitude?"

"WHAT?" asked Marco's father.

Marco gasped and clapped one
hand to his mouth and the other to
his middle. "Dad attitude d.

MS. FARLEY
began to LAUGH,
and she has dimples!
(who knew?)

You got it,
kiddo!
what tipped you off?

"Because you do what you think you should do, and
you don't care what anybody else thinks," I said.

"Well, who does THAT remind me of?" said Marco.

Ms. Farley stood up
and took a bow,
and I bowed
back.

It won't be an A.

It won't be
an F,
either!

Then Marco's father said, "Marco? A few minutes?" which was the signal for Marco to take me into the little studio where all the prismacolor pens lived in gorgeous round trays, each in its own stand. I glowed:

I had accomplished Job **1** (Ms. Farley)

and now I began Job **2** (toolbox)

with Marco (Job **3**) by asking about

Job **4** (what should my Dad do?):

How come your Dad can make $o much moolah graphic designing?

He DOESN'T. It's the books.

Books?

He illustrates book covers. Best sellers. His covers MAKE them best sellers.

Cool!

Gee.

Yeah, but most of the money is from his parents who died.

Oh.

Plus child support from mom.

Yeah, there's money. But so far it's just me and him.

I'd RATHER HAVE MOM THAN CHILD SUPPORT PAYMENTS!

Why do you think he's wild about Sparkle Farkle?

Oh, by the way. I can go to the April Fool Hop.

WHAT? WHEN? WHY?

Good!

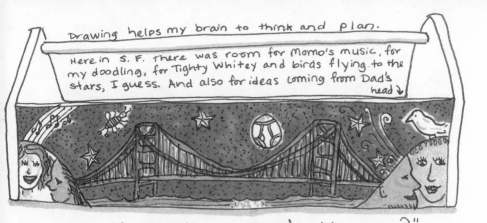

Drawing helps my brain to think and plan.

Here in S.F. there was room for Momo's music, for my doodling, for Tighty Whitey and birds flying to the stars, I guess. And also for ideas coming from Dad's head ↓

Marco said, "So THAT'S what you do with color?"

There was a **KNOCK** on Marco's door and Ms. Farley stuck her head in and I pretended I didn't see her and said, "Don't you know I have a behavior problem?"

"NAH," said Marco, also on purpose. "You just have your own way of doing things. THAT'S for sure."

"Where there's a problem there can be a solution," said

"A **behavior solution**?" I said.

"Yeah, such as the original way you fulfilled your assignment. You'll do fine, even if you drive people crazy sometimes."

I said a brave thing.

TAKES ONE TO KNOW ONE, SPARKLE.

And then I realized something **vital**:

I'm really sorry, Marco. I don't think I can stay for dinner after all.
There's something I need to do.

First I borrowed the phone and called Staci on her cell phone. Then I walked home down the giant hill so I could stop at the art store with my allowance. Then I walked back "home" to Staci's, up her hill one VERY LAST TIME, with my hands full.

I hid the toolbox in an IKEA bag full of clothes that were going to the new house.

I hid the bag from the art store, too.

"Dad, what's the last sculpture you ever thought of making?" I asked.

"Oh, I DUNNO," said Dad.

"No, really. Think!"

He stirred his spaghetti sauce and tasted it and gave me some and asked me if I thought it needed more basil and didn't answer my question. But I went into the living room where Mom and Staci and Momo were listening, and left Dad to stir.

I HOPED SOME IDEAS STARTED STIRRING IN HIS HEAD, too.

Here is what else happened that last night:

1. Mom gave me money to cover what I'd spent at the art store, because she could tell what I was trying to do.

2. Staci gave me a glue gun she said was left over from a project. And glue sticks and two sets of wind-up teeth.

They walk around and chatter, kind of like Momo. HA! Good one!

3. I called Elizabeth. I said, "Can you get WHERE'S WALDO to let us into the new house tomorrow after school, and will you go with me? I have to stop somewhere on the way, too."

She said, "SURE! Sounds MYSTERIOUS. I'm going to be sick tomorrow, though."
I said, "Oh! What's wrong?"
She said, "Nuthin' now." Talk about mysterious.

"WHY don't you go to sleep, Dodo?" asked MOMO.

"WHY don't you go to
sleep, Momohead?"
I asked.

"WHY doesn't everybody go to sleep?" called Mom.
Staci came and put Sven on Momo's and my bed
between us, and he stayed, purrrrrring.

"Where's Dad?" called Momo. All the lights were off
and I was drawing by the feathery light that came
in from the street through the tree and the glow
from the starlights we would have to take down in
the morning, the very last thing.

"WHERE DO YOU THINK I AM?" said Dad.

Momo opened her mouth to answer, and FOR ONCE
in her life, she shut it. She looked at me.
She shrugged. I shrugged back. We didn't know.

She whispered,

WHAT IF in the new house I'm scared
to be in a room and a bed alone?

I said,

If you try getting in bed with ME
with your STINKY feet I will
kick you back out again!

Mom said, You can get in with me, Momo moosh.

Dad didn't say a word. Sven purrrrrrrred.

9. New Place for Our Stars

folded-up star lights

beckoning cat

pajamas etc.

Here they are: my worldly possessions.

All our other stuff was in boxes and bags at the new house.
Almost all. Our things to wear to the
APRIL FOOL HOP were on hangers on
Staci's bathroom door. We had bought
them when we were at Target, in between
the window blinds and my new red stapler.

— BUT FIRST : WORK. SCHOOL. REAL LIFE.

I had a MISSION : to find all the best materials for a
SCULPTURE that I could possibly manage.

Everything else was less important, even the announcements
(Ms. Wu had made me promise I'd do another
announcement today.) Even slow dances.
(My face got red all by itself every time I
thought of Magic Marco, or Ms. Farley
dancing with Marco's dad.) And even the fact that
Elizabeth was coughing, stopped at the water fountain
too much, or putting her head down on her books.

I was too busy collecting things: by lunch I had

Lost & Found items
from Homeroom

a staved-in
sombrero from
Spanish

a spent Slinky
from science

gutted gym gear
from gym
class

patriotic pictures and
paper goods from
social studies

I had all my treasure in a big net bag Ms. Keller lent me. I even got the idea of visiting teachers I didn't have that day to ask for their donations:

big blob of clay from mr. Hill (art)

scrap wood from mr. Chess (shop)

kitchen stuff from Home Arts

I dragged it all into the lunchroom and plopped down at a table to quickly gobble some lunch when...

CocoLilynSasha showed up all covered in **tears** and momo trailing along behind looking worried and who else but the famous singer Elizabeth Colleen Callahan Cootie Catcher who opened her mouth just wide enough to croak out,

Doodlebug?

I said, "You're sick!" She nodded, rolling her eyes.

How can she possibly sing?

WHAT are we gonna do?

She said to find you.

"WHY ME?" I asked.

Cootie Catcher looked at momo, who said

You're the other karaoke official.

So what could I do? "Find a sub!" I told CocoLilynSasha.

I'll admit it, I felt like banging their heads together.

Just ask somebody.

How about Franky?

Well, does one of you want to step up and do it?

oh will somebody tell me why girls are so *girly* ???

I'll do it!

Elizabeth made a little cough. It was making her sick, too!

She croaked, "you all made choir?" They shook their heads.

I'D BE TOO EMBARRASSED.

Said Coco.

I'M NOT GOOD ENOUGH FOR A SOLO.

Said Lily.

FRANKY'S THE REAL SINGER IN MY FAMILY.

Said Sasha.

And then there is the mysterious phenomenon of MOMO.

"**Fine,**" she said in a Confusion. Just make sure you're all there right on time to sing backup on R.E.S.P.E.C.T. Elizabeth put her head down on her arms in the middle of the lunch table. "Cootie Catcher's sick," I said to Coco N Lily N Sasha N Momo. "Why don't you <u>run along</u>?"

ohhhhhh....

ALL RIGHT, Cootie Head, they're gone!

It's gonna —WORK!

Of course she has to go on faking 'til the end of school, but not act sick enough to get sent home or the school rule is she can't go to the dance then.

I just got back to gathering SCULPTURE STUFF until the bell.

I stashed the latest prizes in the string bag:

old vocabulary workbooks from Language Arts

Wordly Wordly Wise

and a creepy styrofoam head, I don't know why Ms. Michaels has it!

a water pot, two brush heads, and some used-up oil-paint tubes from art

I am flat.

a compass and some measurey thingers from math and Mr. Juarez plus an old eraser and those stub pencils some boys like to make.

All the teachers say, "I can't wait to see the sculpture," so that it occurs to me that just because I asked them for old junk that would look cool in a piece of ARTWORK they think I'm going to be the artist. WELL,

I can't worry too much about people's perceptions.

Elizabeth is having the same problem when I meet her.

She is trying to look sick enough not to sing and yet well enough to dance...

Oh my gosh DOODLEBUG get me out of this dramatic NIGHTMARE!

I cannot think yet about what her drama is going to lead to, tonight, for Momo or anybody else.

NEW HOUSE KEY!!!

You're my hero, Cootie Catcher!

There is a lot to do. We go to meet Momo and Cootie Croaks out "PRACTICE 'Take a Chance.' Just in case."

Momo says, "We're supposed to go straight home, Dodo!"

It's time, the April Fool Hop starts at 5. Hurry, hurry.

"Just tell them I had to stay after," I tell her. My parents are used to my staying after at school.

Instead I dash with Elizabeth to the new and cozy little cottage — by way of Chinatown (just one quick stop) and make it home in time to get dressed up.

"What's going on?" I say, dashing into Staci's apartment with my best NO QUESTIONS PLEASE attitude.

Momo was having a **CRISIS.**

She stood staring into the mirror. As usual she had her hairbrush in her hand but she was not singing into it. She was actually brushing her hair with it and she did not like what she was seeing in the mirror.

"Yo, Momo mojo, you look like a **rock star!**"

Nice job, Dodo: the poor kid burst into tears.

"I look **STUPID** in these big polka dots and NOBODY CARES if I go to this dance anyway. CoconLilynSasha think I am just a conceited

 **creep**—"

> They're jealous! You go sing R. E. S. P. E. C. T. and soon they're gonna follow you around.

BEFORE, the plan had been for Mom to drive Momo to Coco's so she could go to the dance with the Cootie-ettes but NOW, Dad was working late so Mom had to drive me and Marco and Elizabeth and Waldo. Plus ALSO, Momo wasn't going to drive with CoconLilynSasha any more so she had to squash in with us. Some DOUBLE DATE!

This is actually me. New hairdo. New outfit.

Marco wore a purple tie.

old hairdo
very pink cheeks

new hairdo

old hairdo

big polo

baggy pants

little dress

little shoes

skate shoes

Elizabeth and Waldo went around holding pinkies all night.

momo and I each had a new charm on our bracelets. mom safety-pinned them on. "Sea lions," she said. "You're real San Franciscans now."

But Dad wasn't home to see us or take pictures or anything. So Staci took some instead, and before we left she took us aside and said,

Quit worrying. It's a new life. Now give **Sven** a kiss and go dancing!

I needed just one more thing from Staci, and she promised to do it. "When Warn gets home, we'll all three go get dim sum in Chinatown. Then they can pick you all up from the dance and you can go home."

I didn't want Mom to go to the new house until Dad was there. "*Thanks!*" I said, and we left.

As we drove away, Staci was going to her car to go pick up Dad from work.

The very instant we stepped through the gym doorway, Marco said an amazing thing:

"Okay, Doodlebug, let's get this SLOW DANCING out of the way!"

I don't know how to draw myself! But I was definitely RIGHT HERE!

Is it even slow dance music?

Nope, it's HIP-HOP. Who cares?

I have to remember 4-EVER how Magic Marco's face looked, slow dancing to FAST music!

And he was right: we relaxed a lot after that!

WHEN I THINK OF THIS NIGHT, THIS IS MY MAIN PICTURE BUT

also...

Mr. Stein danced with me — not a slow dance like with Marco but hand-in-hand spinning around. He called it "swing dancing" and he also did it with Ms. Wu and Lily and Mr. Juarez and Elizabeth and Franky.

Waldo and Cootie did robot dancing.

Thriller started off the famous karaoke kontest with a big bang:

oh, man! oops! other way!

So did Momo and (of all people) Franky!

Some of choir kids sang "Rent."

This song goes out to all the short people!

Yes, Franky blew the roof off with "We Are the Champions."

Queen

But when Momo took the mike and stepped under the mirror ball and the spotlight, it was in my opinion the great musical moment of the night and when she finished singing,

R.E.S.P.E.C.T.!

THE WHOLE PLACE WENT CRAZY!!!!!

AND THEN...

And now...

"Take a chance on me", by ABBA!

Momo was still standing there. The clapping for R.E.S.P.E.C.T. hadn't even stopped yet.

Some of the loudest clappers were Coconlilyn Sasha, and then (if you don't know it, there's only a quick beat before the singer starts singing all alone)

♫ IF YOU CHANGE ♫ YOUR MIND... ♫

and suddenly COCONLily N Sasha changed THEIRS...

♫ Take a Chance!   ♫ Take a Chance!   ♫ Take a chance!

They sounded great.

and Elizabeth's voice cheering them sounded perfectly healthy.

oh, well!

You go girls!!

Did they win the contest? Yeah, they did - tied with Franky and Queen.

And Mom was even there to see momo and the girls get their prizes. Sasha introduced them.

This is Momo

and COCO

and Lolo

and I'm Soso!

The prizes - selected by Mr. Stein - were inflatable microphones.
Everybody got even LOUDER.

ms. Farley and Mom found a quiet spot near the door.

She's got a G- and that's mainly for encouragement.

Hmmmmm.

Didn't they both have enough on their minds tonight without ME?

And now, here it was our first night in our new house and—

Where's Dad?

I asked Mom.

He never made it to the dim sum place.

What about Staci??

She texted me: They were talking.

and also,

CocoaLaLonSazonMomonFranky =☺ wanted to all sleep in sleeping bags on Sasha and Franky's family room floor, and sing and yak and plan until morning.

Oh please, Mrs. Bussey!

We've got lots of room...

...and an extra sleeping bag!

It'll be SO FUN!

PLEASE, mom! Can I?

Let her, ma. She'll be home tomorrow.

WELL, O.K.

But she didn't love it.

AFTER ALL THAT *slow dancing,* a good night hug was easy for Magic Marco and me. I touched his hair with my fingertips: **Soft.**

Then Marco went home with his dad and Ms. Farley.

I thought about Ms. Farley and her attitude. All of a sudden I got an idea:

What if her **Problem** wasn't having an F attitude?

What if her **problem** was that the teacher who gave her the F didn't understand her? Whoa, Nellie.

Mom seemed very uncertain about talking to me.

 What's that G= all about?

she said first, but then she asked gently,

Dodo, did you have a nice time?

I whispered, *yes*  then asked,

Ma, does *understanding* somebody make it **harder** to like them sometimes?

Yup. Then she added, But maybe it makes it **easier** to love them.

 Mom and I drove Waldo and Elizabeth home. They held hands— not just pinkies— in the back seat.

Beltoon

 See you, neighbor!

Mom and I
drove into our new driveway. It was very quiet.

"Have elves been here?" asked Mom

"It was me," I said.

"So you and Momo have claimed the front bedroom?"

"**No!** That's for you and Dad"

"But you hung your stars there"

I said, "No, I got you guys your own stars."

And I wondered:

Were Staci + Sven alone again?

Was Dad there?
Because except for the stars and birds, the house was DARK

On the side of the kitchen there is a laundry room with a table. You come through there when you park the car in the garage. I had it all set up for Dad.

TAKE YOUR TIME

wordly

"It's a SCULPTURE STUDIO," I told Mom. (Ms. Keller gave me the testing-time sign.)

A car door slammed. "YOU show him!" I told Mom. I went upstairs to my new room

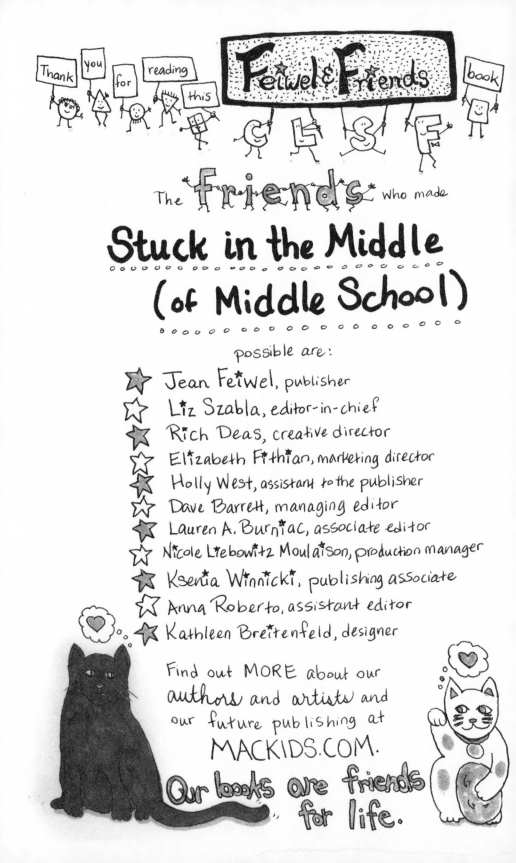

Thank you for reading this Feiwel & Friends book

The **Friends** who made

Stuck in the Middle (of Middle School)

possible are:

⭐ Jean Feiwel, publisher
☆ Liz Szabla, editor-in-chief
⭐ Rich Deas, creative director
☆ Elizabeth Fithian, marketing director
⭐ Holly West, assistant to the publisher
☆ Dave Barrett, managing editor
⭐ Lauren A. Burniac, associate editor
☆ Nicole Liebowitz Moulaison, production manager
⭐ Ksenia Winnicki, publishing associate
☆ Anna Roberto, assistant editor
⭐ Kathleen Breitenfeld, designer

Find out MORE about our authors and artists and our future publishing at MACKIDS.COM.

Our books are friends for life.